# THE HARDCORE WAR

# THE HARDCORE WAR

## AN UNOFFICIAL LEAGUE OF GRIEFERS ADVENTURE, #6

Winter Morgan

Sky Pony Press
New York

Copyright © 2015 by Hollan Publishing, Inc.

Minecraft ® is a registered trademark of Notch Development AB

The Minecraft game is copyright © Mojang AB

Sky Pony Press books may be purchased in bulk at special discounts for sales promotion, corporate gifts, fund-raising, or educational purposes. Special editions can also be created to specifications. For details, contact the Special Sales Department, Sky Pony Press, 307 West 36th Street, 11th Floor, New York, NY 10018 or info@skyhorsepublishing.com.

Sky Pony® is a registered trademark of Skyhorse Publishing, Inc.®, a Delaware corporation.

Minecraft ® is a registered trademark of Notch Development AB
The Minecraft game is copyright © Mojang AB

Visit our website at www.skyponypress.com.

10 9 8 7 6 5 4 3 2 1

Library of Congress Cataloging-in-Publication Data is available on file.

Cover design by Brian Peterson
Cover photograph credit Megan Miller

Print ISBN: 978-1-63450-540-6
Ebook ISBN: 978-1-63450-953-4

Printed in Canada

# TABLE OF CONTENTS

# THE HARDCORE WAR

# 1
# THE HOTEL

Everyone was excited about the opening of the new hotel. Violet had spent months working on the beachfront hotel, located outside of her vibrant and peaceful town. The grand opening attracted people from all around the Overworld. Even some of her old friends showed up. Violet looked into the crowd and spied Will and Trent.

Violet smiled as she stood on the podium and spoke. "Welcome to the grand opening! This hotel is for you."

The crowd cheered. Violet welcomed a steady stream of guests into the new hotel. For the first time in her life, Violet was eager for the night to set in. She wasn't worrying about hostile mobs that might spawn in the dark. She was too busy watching guests arrive and check in to sleep in the hotel's beds, which Violet had crafted.

"We have a huge turnout," remarked Noah, "and so many of our friends showed up. You were right. This was a great idea. Now we have a place where our friends can stay when they visit."

"And we can make new friends by working at the hotel." Violet loved meeting new people, and she figured creating a hotel would be a great way to do so.

Noah agreed. "Yes, and with Daniel behind bars, we will finally be able to enjoy ourselves."

"Let's go say hi to Will and Trent." Violet ran over to her treasure-hunter friends.

Will and Trent stood in the hotel's lobby. Will gave a high five to Violet. "You did a great job. What a grand hotel." Will looked out through the large window toward the blue ocean.

"Thanks! This is all so exciting!" Violet found the entire day invigorating. She was anxious for morning to arrive, when she and Noah would serve the guests cake and ask them how they had enjoyed their first night in the hotel.

Trent joined them and cautioned, "Look out the window. It's getting dark. We should make our way to our rooms."

Violet said good night to her friends. Tonight she wasn't staying in the tree house; she would sleep at the hotel in a comfortable room on the top floor. She opened the door to the room, walked to the window, and watched the sun set.

As Violet climbed into bed, she heard a loud roar and quickly jumped out of bed. Noah rushed into her room. "Violet! Do you see what's outside?"

"Please don't tell me that it's the Ender Dragon!" Violet pleaded.

"I'm afraid so," Noah replied, and he led Violet down the hall to the stairs. They raced out of the hotel, armed with snowballs and their bows and arrows.

"Violet!" Hannah called out. "What's happening? Why is the Ender Dragon flying through town?"

Ben jogged over and said, "I just checked. Daniel is in his jail cell, so this can't be his handiwork."

"It doesn't matter who summoned the Ender Dragon," Violet exclaimed. "We just have to destroy it!"

The mammoth dragon flew by the hotel. The dragon's enormous, black, scaly wing struck the side of the hotel, crashing into the lobby window and shattering the glass. Violet was devastated. Hotel guests ran toward the exit in terror.

"Help!" the guests cried in unison.

Violet, Noah, Ben, and Hannah staged an attack on the hostile mob from the End. Will and Trent joined their friends in the battle against the Ender Dragon. The fiery beast roared and lunged at the gang. Noah struck the dragon with an arrow, which diminished the health bar of the flying terror.

Violet heaved a snowball that landed on the dragon's face. This infuriated the dragon, and it charged at Violet. She fumbled with her bow and arrow, but then the beast flung Violet into the air.

As Violet flew through the night sky, Noah pounded the purple-eyed dragon with arrows, further diminishing its health bar. Violet landed on the ground, quickly regaining her footing and shooting arrows at the dragon.

The dragon roared and flew into the hotel, breaking another window. But the beast was no match for the growing number of people who aimed their bows and arrows at it. Violet smiled when she saw the hotel guests join her friends in battle.

Beams of light flashed from the dragon's body as the beast exploded.

"There's an End portal over there," Will said as he pointed at the portal and the dragon egg. "Should we go to the End?"

Noah stared at the portal. He felt conflicted; he wasn't sure why they should travel to the End. If they did, they'd surely have to battle yet another Ender Dragon.

"What should we do?" asked Violet.

Everyone was confused; they weren't sure what to do next.

"I don't think we should go," objected Trent. "We have to stay here and figure out who summoned the Ender Dragon."

"I agree," Violet replied, as she looked at the broken window in the lobby and realized she had to rebuild part of the hotel.

The group walked away from the End portal and headed back to the hotel. As they approached the entrance, a horde of zombies lumbered across the sandy beach and plodded into the lobby.

"Zombie attack!" Will shouted.

The exhausted hotel guests took out their diamond swords and bows and arrows. The zombies ripped the doors from hotel rooms and lunged at the guests, but the vacant-eyed undead mob was attacked by a slew of arrows. Violet dashed behind a zombie and destroyed it with her diamond sword.

When the hotel was free of zombies, Violet told the hotel guests, "Thank you for your help. You saved the hotel. But we must all get to our beds and sleep. We need to rest."

The guests nodded in agreement and returned to their rooms.

"Are you going up to bed?" asked Noah. "Or should we stay up and keep a lookout for hostile mobs?"

Violet said, "I think we should get some sleep. If we don't, we'll never have enough strength to battle whoever is behind this evil attack on the hotel."

Violet retired to her hotel room and took a sip of milk to restore her energy. She crawled into bed but couldn't sleep; she was too restless trying to figure out who had staged the attack on the hotel. With Daniel in the jailhouse, the townspeople had enjoyed a period of peace, but now that was being destroyed. She wondered if Daniel might be able to conduct this attack from his jail cell and if he had access to command blocks.

As Violet began drifting off to sleep, she heard a familiar voice scream, "Help!"

# 2

# JAILBREAK

Violet rushed out the door. Outside her hotel room, she saw Noah battling Daniel in the hallway.

"How did you escape?" Violet asked as she lunged toward Daniel with her diamond sword.

"Like I'd tell you how I did it!" Daniel laughed as he struck Noah.

Hotel guests opened their doors to see the commotion in the hallway. One of the guests shot an arrow at Daniel. Another guest slammed his sword against Daniel's armored body. Despite the armor, the strikes weakened Daniel, and he fumbled for some milk. Before he could sip the milk, though, a person wearing a black helmet ran down the hall.

Daniel called out to the helmeted man, "Come over here, Thomas!"

"You need help fighting your own battle?" Thomas asked scornfully as he walked toward Daniel.

"Yes, I do," admitted Daniel.

As Thomas struck Noah with his sword, he shouted a warning: "I have put everyone on Hardcore mode. So there is no respawning for anyone. Say good-bye!"

"What?" Daniel sounded shocked. He didn't have a lot of milk or potions of healing in his inventory, and he didn't want to be destroyed in Hardcore mode. If you were destroyed in Hardcore mode, the game was over.

Thomas's evil laugh pierced everyone's ears. "I am going to destroy everyone in the Overworld. There is no saving you. This is a battle to the end."

Everyone was surprised when Daniel pleaded with his friend, "You have to change the settings. You must take us off Hardcore mode."

"Never!" Thomas screamed. He delivered a final blow to a hotel guest, who disappeared. Violet shrieked in horror. Before she could strike Thomas with her sword, he threw a potion of invisibility on himself. All that remained was a piece of wool.

"He's escaped!" Violet called out. "Hey! Why is there a piece of wool here?" She picked up the wool and broke it into pieces.

"Who was that person terrorizing us?" Noah asked Daniel.

Daniel stuttered, "Um-m, Thomas—he helped me escape."

Violet asked, "How do you know him?"

"He is a griefer," Daniel replied. "He also freed the others in the jail."

Violet imagined the rainbow griefers sprinting around the town, causing havoc and seeking revenge on the townspeople who had imprisoned them. She feared they'd destroy the townspeople, not realizing the world had been changed to Hardcore mode. Violet's heart beat fast. She was very worried. She also feared that a naturally spawned hostile mob attack might end her life.

"We have to change the setting from Hardcore mode!" Violet shouted at Daniel.

"I don't have any control over this. Thomas is the one who set everyone to Hardcore mode," Daniel replied.

"Where is Thomas?" Noah pointed his sword at Daniel and warned, "If I destroy you with this sword, you won't respawn. You had better help us. Your evil friend has the potential to annihilate the entire population of the Overworld."

Daniel agreed with Noah. "I want to stop Thomas, too, but I don't have any idea where he's hiding."

The rainbow griefers that were released from prison emerged from the stairway and stormed toward Violet and her friends. Violet was surprised when Daniel ordered them to stop: "Put your swords and arrows down. Thomas set the Overworld to Hardcore mode. We need to conserve our energy."

The rainbow griefers listened. An orange griefer asked, "What should we do?"

Daniel announced, "Drink or eat whatever you can—you need to make sure your food and energy bar is full. We want to be prepared for any type of attack."

As those words left Daniel's mouth, four zombies spawned at the end of the hallway and lumbered forward.

Hotel guests ran to their rooms for shelter, but the zombies ripped the doors from their hinges.

The guests shot arrows at the zombies. Violet and her friends attacked the undead mob. Noah watched as Daniel joined them in the battle against the zombies. Daniel struck a zombie with his diamond sword and destroyed the vacant-eyed creature.

"We need to find Thomas," Daniel said to Noah.

Once the zombies were defeated, Noah said, "Daniel, you have destroyed our Olympic games and our amusement park. Now you expect us to listen to you?"

"But we must work together to find Thomas," explained Daniel.

"Work together?" Noah couldn't believe Daniel had uttered those words.

A green creeper silently lurked down the hotel hallway, slinking up behind a purple rainbow griefer.

"Watch out!" shouted Violet.

The purple griefer didn't hear Violet.

*Kaboom!*

The creeper exploded, and the purple griefer was destroyed, too.

Daniel stared ahead. "We have to do something about being stuck on Hardcore mode. If we don't, this will be the end of all of us."

Violet held her sword to Daniel's chest. "We will take care of Thomas. You have to go back to jail. We don't trust you, so we can't work with you."

"I'm not going back to jail!" Daniel yelled defiantly. He was infuriated.

Ben and Hannah hurried down the hallway. They joined Noah and Violet and surrounded Daniel.

Noah said, "Daniel, this is our battle. We fight for justice."

Daniel realized that with just a few strikes from each of their swords, he could be destroyed. He put his head down and submitted. "Okay, I'll go back to jail."

The sun rose as Daniel and the rainbow griefers left the hotel. They were escorted toward the jail.

# 3

# DEFAULT SETTINGS

The town broke out in chaos as the gang marched Daniel and the rainbow griefers back to the jailhouse.

Valentino the Butcher emerged from his shop and called out, "People are disappearing and not coming back!"

Townspeople gathered in the center square and watched as Daniel and the griefers marched into the secure building.

When the group entered the jailhouse, Violet noticed wool on the ground. She picked it up and noted, "That's odd. There's more wool here."

Noah led Daniel into his cell and told him, "You're home."

"Very funny," Daniel remarked. As Noah closed the gates to the jail cell, Daniel said, "You must find Thomas."

"We will," replied Noah.

"Be honest with us, Daniel," demanded Violet. "Do you know where Thomas is hiding? We need to know."

"I would check in the ocean. He's an expert at surviving underwater," suggested Daniel. "But I'm not certain he's there. He is a very tricky person."

Violet agreed. "Thomas must be tricky. He helped you escape from jail."

"Yes," Daniel added. "He isn't an easy person to fight. He's very skilled, so you better be careful."

Outside the prison, the townspeople analyzed the situation. They were curious why people were being destroyed and not respawning in their beds.

Valentino called to Noah, "Why are people disappearing?"

Noah explained that everyone was set to Hardcore mode so they couldn't respawn. The people began to talk all at once, with no one listening to anyone else. The crowd agreed the situation was awful, and they were scared.

The townspeople were mad. They wanted to destroy Daniel. One person shouted, "We must destroy this evil menace that set us to Hardcore mode!" They forced their way into the jailhouse.

"Stop!" Noah called out. "Daniel isn't the one who put us on Hardcore mode."

Valentino asked, "We have another enemy? Who is it?"

"His name is Thomas. He's another griefer, and he lives beneath the ocean."

"You must stop him," Valentino pleaded with the group of friends.

Noah replied, "We are going to travel to the Ocean Biome to search for Thomas. But we want everyone to be careful while we are away. Remember to never let your energy level get too low, and try to stay indoors."

The townspeople discussed together how they would stay safe, until one of them cried out in pain, "Ouch!"

Noah saw two skeletons standing by the street lined with village shops. "Skeletons? In daylight?" he said.

"Someone must have summoned them," Violet said as she pulled back and released an arrow at a skeleton.

"I'm sure it was Thomas!" exclaimed Noah.

"And look!" Hannah cried out in terror. "There's a spider jockey, too!"

A skeleton shot arrows while riding the black, red-eyed spider. Violet shielded herself from the skeleton attack while she continued trying to destroy the spider jockey.

"Shoot the skeleton!" Hannah called to Violet. "You have him in sight. Do it now!"

Violet aimed at the spider jockey, but she missed. "It's moving too fast!"

Ben bravely dashed toward a skeleton with his diamond sword and destroyed it.

Hannah noticed his small victory and cheered, "Good job, Ben! Now, please help us!"

Ben joined Violet and Hannah to battle the spider jockey. An arrow flew with dead aim from his bow, and it struck the spider, obliterating it.

Hannah rushed toward a skeleton and shot an arrow. "I got it!" she shouted, and the skeleton was destroyed.

Once the hostile mobs were gone, Violet looked at the jailhouse. She saw Daniel peering through his jail cell window. Violet peered right back through the window. "If I find you were behind this attack, I *will* destroy you."

Daniel was angry. "I wasn't behind this attack. I wanted to help you battle the skeletons, so you wouldn't be destroyed, but I'm helpless because I'm in this jail cell."

"Helpless?" Violet laughed. "And you wanted to *help* us? I don't believe you."

Noah walked over and confronted him. "Daniel, you were constantly threatening to put us on Hardcore mode, so how can we believe you now care to help us?"

Daniel paused, and then replied, "I think being in this jail cell has changed me. I've watched your townspeople every day as they pass my window and are friendly to each other, and I've grown to like it here. I felt guilty when I saw some of your townspeople destroyed as Thomas helped me escape. And I was devastated when I found out they wouldn't respawn. That is pure evil."

"Wow, if you think someone is evil, they must be really bad," Violet said. She didn't know if she and her friends should trust Daniel, but she did know they had to find Thomas, and they had to do it quickly.

"We have to go," Noah told her. "If we don't stop Thomas, he might summon more mobs, and we won't be able to survive multiple attacks. The odds are against us. We were lucky this time." And without a second thought about Daniel, they turned and walked away from the prison.

The gang was ready to set out for the Ocean Biome. They walked toward the shorefront hotel. The guests had assembled in the lobby to figure out a plan for survival. Now that the Overworld was on Hardcore mode, everyone was looking out for each other. They needed to make sure they were all safe and wouldn't be destroyed. The hotel guests decided to stay in the hotel until the world was safe again.

One hotel guest told Violet and her friends, "I know Thomas. I think I can help you."

"You know Thomas?" Violet asked.

"Yes, he was once a good friend of mine."

"Who are you?" she pressed him.

"My name is Adam. I come from Thomas's town."

"Do you have any idea where he might be?" asked Noah.

"I can't say for certain, but I can tell you that he is extremely tricky and smart."

"We've heard that before," Noah noted. "I think you should come with us, though. Any help is great."

Adam added, "I'm an alchemist. I have a bunch of potions that might come in handy, too."

"Is there anything else you can tell us about Thomas that might be helpful?" asked Hannah.

"Yes, he likes to dig and hide in tunnels. He also likes to leave a mark. Last time he left wool whenever he griefed someone," replied Adam.

"I found wool in the hallway of the hotel and also at the jailhouse!" exclaimed Violet.

"That is Thomas's mark!" cried Adam. "I must help you guys find him."

The gang walked toward the edge of the shore. Adam handed everyone a potion of water breathing, and they all dove into the deep blue water.

# 4
# OCEAN BLUE

The group swam through the water searching for Thomas. Violet pointed out an ocean monument not far away. Before the gang could explore the monument, though, they heard a loud growl.

"Oh no!" Hannah called out.

A one-eyed blue guardian swam toward them. The guardian's tail swung back and forth as the evil fish shot a laser at Hannah. The laser turned from purple to yellow.

"I've been struck!" Hannah cried. "I'm very tired. I don't feel well."

"It's Mining Fatigue." Adam handed Hannah some milk, which made her feel better after she drank it.

Noah shot an arrow that struck the guardian and weakened the hostile creature who was guarding the ocean monument. Adam shot more arrows at the fish until it was destroyed.

The gang entered the ocean monument, keeping a close eye out for any guardians that might be swimming nearby.

"I think I see an elder guardian!" Hannah called out to the group. The one-eyed fish swam into the temple. Hannah quickly hid behind a pillar—she didn't want to be the victim of another attack.

"Maybe we shouldn't be searching an ocean monument right now," said Violet. "This is too risky. We need to keep searching for Thomas."

Adam swam next to Violet. He pointed to the floor of the monument and called out, "Look down!"

There was a small hole in the floor. Violet hollered back, "Do you think it's the entrance to a tunnel?"

Adam nodded his head. "This looks like the sort of tunnel Thomas would dig," he replied.

"No!" Ben shouted as he attempted to swim away from the blue guardian with the yellow laser, but it was too late. He was struck.

Adam handed Ben milk. "I don't have much milk left. We must find Thomas and stop the Hardcore mode now. This is getting too dangerous."

Violet's heart skipped a beat when she watched Adam swim toward the hole in the ground. She was afraid that if they got stuck in the tunnel, a hostile creature would destroy them.

"This is the only way we can find Thomas," Adam reassured the group as they followed him into the tunnel.

The tunnel was very long, and they seemed to swim forever. Violet said, "I hope we don't lose too much energy from swimming."

"I'm worried we'll run out of water breathing potion first." Adam checked his inventory as they approached the end of the tunnel.

"A door!" Hannah swam to the entrance and opened it.

The doorway led to a cavernous room filled with gold bars. "I bet this is where Thomas stores his loot. He can't be far from here."

Two guardians weaved through the stacks of gold bars and aimed their lasers at Violet and Noah. Adam and Ben shot arrows at the guardians, while Violet and Noah tried to shield themselves from the attack.

Adam handed the two friends the last of the milk. Suddenly, he spotted Thomas swimming in the distance.

"I see Thomas!" exclaimed Adam.

The group swam toward Thomas as he left the gold storage room through another door.

"Thomas!" Adam called out. "Stop! You can't get away with this."

The evil griefer turned back and laughed, "I think I already have."

Thomas took out a potion of invisibility and splashed it on himself. He could no longer be seen and escaped again. The group was upset to lose him, and they were also running low on their potion of water breathing.

Violet noticed a block of wool on the floor, but she didn't pick it up. She was in a rush to get out of the water before the potion for water breathing wore off.

"We have to swim to the surface," Noah gasped. He could barely breathe. The group swam back through the tunnel and into the ocean monument. They needed to get out of the monument and into the open water quickly so they could swim to the surface.

Violet felt defeated as she reached the shore. The hotel guests hurried out to greet them.

"Are we still on Hardcore mode?" one guest asked Violet.

Violet looked down at her feet in the wet sand. She didn't want to reply. The answer would only disappoint the hotel guests. "I'm sorry. We saw Thomas, but we weren't able to change the settings. We are very upset."

The sky turned dark and rain began to pound the shoreline. The hotel guests ran into the lobby to avoid getting drenched. Just then, a horde of skeletons spawned on the shore and attacked the guests fleeing into the hotel.

Violet and Noah ignored the rain and struck the skeletons with their diamond swords. Hannah and Ben shot arrows at the creatures. Adam splashed potions on the bony beasts as rain fell from the sky.

Two skeletons cornered Hannah against a tree, and she panicked. Hannah cried to the others for help, but they were all busy fighting their own skeleton battles. Hannah struck one of the skeletons with her diamond sword, but the other skeleton hit her. She was rapidly losing hearts, and her energy and health bars were dangerously low. Hannah used her last bit of energy to destroy one of the skeletons, but she couldn't fight anymore.

"I'm here!" Ben called out, and he struck the skeleton a final blow. Hannah was safe.

Adam rushed over and gave Hannah a potion of healing. She thanked him and admitted, "I don't know how much longer we can battle these hostile mobs while we're on Hardcore mode."

Ben and Adam agreed. Something had to be done.

Adam said, "I've defeated Thomas before. He isn't going to win. We just have to find out where he's hiding and change the setting."

"You make it sound so easy," sighed Hannah.

Violet called out to her friends, "Don't just stand around and talk. We need help. There are still two skeletons left."

Ben, Adam, and Hannah ran toward their friends and helped them defeat the remaining skeletons. Once all of the skeletons were obliterated, Adam said something that shocked everyone: "We are running low on resources. I think we have to travel to the Nether to get more Nether wart to brew potions."

"Not the Nether!" Violet dreaded the thought of going to the Nether.

"He's right. We need to go to the Nether," Hannah said. She was a potion expert and knew they needed supplies if they were ever going to win this battle.

Adam began to build a portal. "It's the only way we can survive," he conceded.

Purple mist rose through the air as the group hopped onto the portal and began their journey to the Nether.

# 5
# NETHERMIND

iolet looked up at the sky, searching for ghasts and blazes. "We have to be very careful," she reminded her friends.

"This will be a quick trip," Adam reassured her. "We will just get the supplies we need for potions and then head back to town."

A zombie pigman walked by them, but the group didn't make eye contact as they trekked through the red Nether landscape. Violet would be the first to admit she didn't want to be in the Nether, but she couldn't help stopping to admire a lava waterfall.

"There is something very beautiful about this waterfall," remarked Violet.

Hannah walked over to gaze at the attraction with Violet. "You're right," she agreed.

Violet glanced down at the edge of the lava-filled river and spotted a block of wool. "Oh my!" she said, pointing at it.

Hannah retrieved the wool and broke it apart. "What is this?"

Violet said, "I think Thomas is in the Nether."

Noah, Ben, and Adam heard her and hurried over. Noah asked, "Did you say Thomas is in the Nether?"

"I think so," Violet said. She pointed to the wool Hannah had found.

"Where can he be hiding?" asked Ben.

Adam answered, "It doesn't matter. We need to find a Nether fortress. That's usually where you can get Nether wart."

"That's easier said than done," Violet said. "It's hard to find a Nether fortress. And we really have to find Thomas. If we don't, we'll never get off Hardcore mode."

A high-pitched shriek split the air, and Noah looked up. "A ghast!" he shouted. He grabbed a snowball from his inventory and aimed it at the fiery beast.

"Watch out!" Violet screamed, and Noah raced away from the fireball the ghast shot at him.

Ben and Adam also threw snowballs at the ghast. After several hits, it was destroyed.

The ghast dropped a tear, and Adam rushed over to pick it up. "This ghast tear is essential for brewing a potion of regeneration," he told the others.

"I'm glad you are getting resources for potions. But I still believe we are wasting too much energy here." Violet was annoyed. She really didn't want to be in the Nether.

Noah continued to lead the group forward. While they walked, Violet listed the reasons she disliked the Nether: "There is no day or night, and the hostile mobs

are much more deadly than the ones in the Overworld."
She was about to list a bunch more reasons why she hated
the Nether when Hannah interrupted her.

"Enough, Violet. Nobody wants to be here. But
Adam and I are alchemists and we can't help everyone
with our potions if we don't have any ingredients to brew
with."

Violet remained quiet as they walked along the
ground made up of netherrack and past more lava rivers.

Noah called out, "I think I see a Nether fortress in
the distance!"

Adam rushed ahead and shouted, "You're right! It is
a Nether fortress."

The group sprinted toward the fortress, but a Nether
brick fence surrounded it. Noah took out his pickaxe and
began to knock down the fence. The others joined him.
As Hannah banged her pickaxe against the fence, she
spotted another block of wool.

"Wool!" Hannah cried out.

"I'll bet Thomas is hiding in this fortress," Adam said
as he knocked down the fence with his pickaxe.

The gang entered the fortress cautiously. Hannah
and Adam looked for soul sand and Nether wart by the
stairs. Noah wanted to search for treasure, but instead he
inspected the floor for tunnels.

"We found Nether wart!" Hannah called to the others. The gang joined them and helped gather the Nether
wart and place it in their inventories.

As they readied themselves to exit the Nether fortress,
four magma cubes bounced in their direction. Violet

grabbed her sword and hit a cube. Hannah attacked the smaller cubes that had broken off the large magma cube.

The gang waged a battle with the cubes, which they had to win quickly. They were losing hearts, and everyone's food bar was low. It was a race against time. One by one, as each magma cube was defeated, Adam grabbed the magma cream that dropped on the ground.

"I can use this magma cream to brew potions of fire resistance," he told them once they had defeated all the magma cubes.

"That's great," Violet said quietly. She wanted Adam to stop talking about the potions he could brew. She wanted them to leave the fortress and to start building a portal that would bring them back to the Overworld.

Two blazes flew toward them and the group dashed out of the fortress.

"We need to build a portal, now!" Violet called out.

The gang threw snowballs at the blazes. As Noah began to construct the portal, Violet noticed a block of wool on the ground. She was about to pick it up when Noah called out, "Quick, Violet! The portal is closing!"

# 6
# RAINBOW REBELS

The group emerged in the center of town just as a roar rippled the air above them.

"An Ender Dragon!" Violet screamed in terror.

"Thomas!" Adam shouted.

Thomas was standing by the village shops, laughing and striking townspeople with his diamond sword. As the Ender Dragon flew toward the gang, Thomas splashed the potion of invisibility on himself and disappeared. Violet sprinted to the jailhouse to see if Daniel was still in his cell. As she approached the jail, she spotted a block of wool.

"Violet!" Daniel called from the window of his jail cell. "Let me out," he pleaded.

"You know I can't do that," Violet said as she drank milk to regain her strength before beginning to battle the Ender Dragon.

"Thomas summoned the Ender Dragon. And I think he is summoning a Wither, too," Daniel told her.

"We'll stop him," Violet said as she shot an arrow at the Ender Dragon, which was lunging into Valentino's butcher shop.

Valentino called out, "My shop!" But he knew there was much more to be lost now that the world was set to Hardcore mode. He could rebuild the shop, but if he was destroyed, he'd never respawn.

The townspeople fought together, using all the supplies they had on hand to destroy the Ender Dragon. Arrows and snowballs flew through the air. The Ender Dragon let out another roar and swung its large scaly wing into the jailhouse. The wing created a gaping hole in the side of the building, and the rainbow griefers escaped from their cells.

Violet wanted to go after the escaped griefers because she knew they would start to attack the townspeople. She ran toward them, but stopped when she saw a purple griefer take out a bow and arrow and shoot at the Ender Dragon. The escaped griefers were joining the townspeople in battle. Daniel also made his way out of the jailhouse through a hole in his cell wall.

Violet and her friends were shocked when they saw Daniel race toward the dragon and strike it with his diamond sword, delivering the final blow to the beast.

"I can't believe I'm about to say this," Violet said as she walked over to Daniel, "but good job."

"I told you. I want to redeem myself and help you defeat Thomas. This is my fault. I started all of this. I'm the one who found Thomas and asked him to come here and break me out of jail. We had a plan to attack the

Overworld together. But I would never have been so cruel as he's been. I'd never set the entire Overworld to Hardcore mode and put everyone in jeopardy."

Now that Daniel had escaped, and the jailhouse was destroyed, the gang had to figure out what they should do with him. They weren't sure if they should build another structure to confine Daniel or if they should let him join them in a battle against Thomas.

Noah admitted to Daniel, "You saved us." He looked at the others as he said, "I think you can help us."

"How?" Daniel asked. He was clearly eager to help. Daniel smiled. Violet looked at Daniel's grin and didn't recognize him, because she had never seen him smile like that before.

"You need to think like a criminal—that will work to our advantage," Noah told Daniel.

Daniel said, "Thomas and I had a plan." He took a deep breath and continued, "It was very evil, and I'm afraid he might go through with it."

"Tell us the plan," Violet demanded.

"First, we were going to blow up the hotel, and then we were going to obliterate your town and leave the town uninhabitable, so you could never rebuild."

"Blow up the hotel!" Violet gasped.

Hannah cried, "If that happens, everyone in the village will be destroyed and will never respawn!"

The sky was growing dark, so the gang headed for the hotel. The guests would be surprised to see Daniel and the rainbow griefers joining them. As night set in, a group of zombies spawned in front of them. Daniel struck a zombie with his diamond sword. Adam threw potions on the undead creatures. Violet used her bow and arrow to annihilate a bunch of zombies.

"Watch out!" Hannah called to an orange griefer as two zombies lunged at him.

Ben destroyed one of the zombies while the orange griefer attacked the other one. The battle was weakening the gang. They just wanted to make their way back to the hotel. They needed to warn the guests that the hotel might explode at any minute.

The last of the zombies was finally destroyed, and the group ran to the hotel. The guests were asleep, and the lobby was empty. Noah lit a torch and placed it on the wall outside the hotel.

Violet noticed a block of wool. "Oh no!" She pointed to the wool.

A creeper snuck up silently behind Violet, but Noah screamed a warning, and Violet was able to escape the blast from it before destroying it with her diamond sword.

"There's wool here!" Violet called to her friends.

Adam walked over to examine the wool and said, "I bet there is also TNT in the hotel."

Daniel inspected the wall around the hotel. He searched around the entire building and shouted, "I see TNT!"

The group began to collect the TNT bricks. Hannah remarked, "I wonder who Thomas has working with him. He couldn't do this alone. There is a lot of TNT here, and he also is summoning the Ender Dragon. That's too much for one person."

"Do you know anyone who might be working with Thomas?" Violet asked Daniel.

He paused to think and replied, "No, I have no idea. I just dealt with him alone."

After the TNT was placed safely in everyone's inventory, Violet took one last walk around the hotel. She passed the front entrance and spotted a piece of wool. "I didn't see that before, did you?" she asked the others.

"No," Ben said as he looked at the wool.

Hannah saw a hole in the ground near the block of wool. "I didn't notice that hole, either."

"A hole?" Violet called out. "Where?"

Adam examined the hole. "I think we have to go down and see if Thomas is there."

"Oh no, not again!" Violet was still recovering from the events in the tunnel in the ocean, but she knew they had to search for Thomas. She drew a deep breath and descended into the hole.

# 7
# HOLES

The tunnel wasn't as long as they had imagined. Within minutes, the gang reached the end.

"There's no door!" Hannah was shocked.

"I bet this is a trap!" Ben called out.

Violet banged her pickaxe against the blocks at the end of the tunnel and broke away the pieces.

"Why are you digging? Shouldn't we just go back the way we came?" asked Hannah.

"Let's see if there is another tunnel that was blocked up here," Violet replied. She banged the pickaxe several times, but there was nothing more.

Noah stood next to Violet. "I think we should head back. This isn't going to end well. This might be a trap Thomas has set up."

"What if he throws bricks of TNT into this tunnel and blows us all to pieces?" Hannah's voice quavered as she spoke.

"I don't think there is any more TNT," said Daniel.

Noah took out his sword and held it against Daniel's chest. "Are you tricking us?"

"No!" cried Daniel. "I just thought we collected all the TNT. Maybe this was an escape tunnel Thomas was building and he didn't have a chance to complete it."

"Or maybe Hannah was right and he is going to blow us up!" shouted Noah.

"I don't know," Daniel said with a frown. "You could be right."

Violet ordered, "We need to get out of here."

The group hurried out of the tunnel, pushing past hotel guests who crowded around the entrance. As the gang climbed out of the hole, the sun began to rise.

Noah spoke in front of the crowd. "We need to come up with a plan. We have to find a way to defeat Thomas." He looked over at Daniel and asked, "Is there anything else you two were planning?"

Before Daniel could answer, a three-headed Wither flew past the hotel, and an Ender Dragon followed it.

"This looks like one of your old tricks!" Noah screamed at Daniel, and he grabbed one of the last snowballs from his inventory.

"But I'm not behind this. Thomas is just mimicking my type of attacks," Daniel protested. He grabbed his bow and arrow and shot at the beast. "I promise to join you in battle."

The Wither shot skulls at the group while the hotel guests tried to avoid being struck, but the skulls destroyed two guests.

"No!" One of the guests screamed out in horror.

Noah threw the last snowball. "This is awful, and we are seriously fighting to the end. Once people get destroyed in this battle, it's over."

The stakes were high, and Violet was fearless as she dashed in front of the Ender Dragon and threw a snowball at the beast. The snowball hit it square in the side, weakening the once-powerful dragon.

Hannah and Ben ran to Violet's side and also threw snowballs and shot arrows at the beast. The strikes were diminishing the dragon's power.

Hannah said, "We don't have that much longer before it's gone. But I don't think I can fight any more. I have no energy left. My health bar is too low."

Adam rushed to Hannah. "Drink this. It will make you stronger."

Hannah drank the potion as she carefully dodged a wither skull that rocketed by her arm.

Daniel's energy was incredibly low, too, but he stepped in front of the dragon and struck the beast with his sword. The dragon exploded, and a portal to the End appeared by the hotel entrance.

Daniel headed over to the portal. Noah warned, "You can't go on that portal. If we travel to the End, it will really be over."

The Wither flew close to Daniel. He didn't have the energy to fight the flying hostile creature. It shot a wither skull at him. He was about to give up and accept the end. He didn't have any tricks up his sleeve, and he was running low on resources. As the wither skull flew in his direction, Violet shouted, "Move!"

Daniel jumped back, narrowly avoiding the strike from the skull. Noah and Violet shot the Wither with arrows and the three-headed beast was destroyed. It dropped a Nether star, which Noah picked up and placed in his inventory.

Violet looked up and said in relief, "The sky is clear."

"We still need to find Thomas," declared Adam.

Daniel shocked everyone when he announced, "I have a confession. I actually know where Thomas is hiding. But I don't have any the energy to travel there. I'm afraid this is the end for me."

Adam confronted Daniel with an offer. "I will give you this potion only if you lead us to Thomas."

Violet added, "I can't believe you knew where he was all this time and you didn't tell us. You lied to us!"

"I'm sorry." Daniel's voice was weak. "I wanted to tell you, but I wasn't sure I could trust you. I thought you might destroy me because of all the things I had done to you guys. I needed to see that we could work together."

"Trust us?" Noah questioned with a laugh.

"I'm sorry," Daniel repeated.

Adam handed Daniel the potion of healing, and he drank it quickly. Adam demanded, "Now tell us where Thomas is hiding."

"I'll admit I'm not one hundred percent certain, but I almost positive he's hiding in a cave in the jungle."

"Which jungle?" Violet asked. "There are many jungles in the Overworld. We need to find out where he is soon before one of us gets destroyed and we never respawn."

"It's the jungle right outside your town," said Daniel.

"We'd better get going, then," said Noah.

"We can head into the Grassy Biome, go past the pastures, and reach the jungle quickly," suggested Ben.

Some of the hotel guests wanted to join the group of friends in the search of Thomas. Violet told them, "We'd love your help, but I think it's best if you stay here. We don't want to lose any more people."

Noah warned the crowd, "Be on the lookout in case Thomas returns. And please come and get us if you see him. We need to work together."

The guests agreed to watch for Thomas. The reformed rainbow griefers also promised to help battle Thomas if he appeared anywhere near the hotel.

So the gang began their trek to the jungle. As Violet hiked, she kept her head down and searched for holes in the ground. She didn't want to miss any secret tunnels.

# 8
# CREEPERS, ENDERMEN, AND ZOMBIES

T he cave should be right over here," Daniel said as he led the group to a lush section of the jungle. Huge green leaves shaded the path. Daniel sheared the leaves and looked for the cave.

"I don't see anything," Adam said as he stood next to Daniel.

"It should be here. This is where Thomas told me he was setting up his headquarters." Daniel hunted nervously for the cave.

"Do you think he might have tricked you?" asked Noah.

"But we were supposed to be working together." Daniel seemed troubled.

"He might have moved locations," suggested Violet. She searched for the cave in the hilly stretch of the jungle, but all she could find were cocoa plants and melons.

"That's true," Daniel said as he paced. "Maybe he's in the Taiga Biome. He loved living in the mountains."

Violet picked some melons and offered them to the group. "We need to eat and be on top of our food bar. If not, we will surely be destroyed."

The gang stopped and devoured the lush melons; they were tasty. Hannah said, "It feels like forever since we were able to relax and just enjoy ourselves."

"I know, but how can we have fun when we have to fight to survive? One wrong move and we can be destroyed," Noah reminded Hannah.

"Yes, this isn't the time for fun and games," added Violet.

Hannah smiled at the group. "At least we can enjoy this melon. Despite all this craziness, I am really happy that I'm with you all. It's great knowing that there are people who like to help each other."

Daniel added, "I have spent such a long time trying to destroy you, and now I realize what a mistake I've made. I'm really enjoying being with you all."

"That means a lot," Violet said to Daniel. "It's very hard to change, and you seem to be doing an excellent job."

Noah glanced at Violet. He was clearly still suspicious of Daniel, but he knew they needed his help. He hoped Violet was correct in trusting Daniel. Noah said, "I hope you see how important friends are and you don't ruin it."

"I won't. I promise," Daniel told the group.

"It's easier said than done," Noah replied. Then he added, "We have to find Thomas. The melon was excellent, but we have a person who is trying to destroy our world and he is loose in the Overworld. We need to find him."

The gang left the jungle. As they made their way toward the mountainous Taiga Biome, Hannah called out, "A creeper!"

A creeper was silently lurking by a big tree. Noah took out his bow and arrow and struck the creeper with one shot.

*Kaboom!* The creeper exploded.

Hannah asked, "Do you think we'll see more hostile mobs as we get closer to Thomas?"

"We have to be prepared for anything," Noah advised.

"I see Endermen," Violet's voice shook. "This must be Thomas's doing. It's too light out for Endermen to spawn without help."

"He's summoning mobs," noted Daniel. "Don't engage the Endermen. Maybe they'll just pass by and not bother us."

The gang tried to avoid eye contact with the two Endermen carrying blocks, but the Endermen noticed them and began to shriek and teleport toward them.

"Help!" Hannah cried as an Enderman teleported in front of her.

"Run toward the water!" shouted Daniel.

A winding river appeared in the distance. Hannah didn't know if she would make it, but she knew she had to try or she would be destroyed forever.

The Enderman was right behind her as she raced as fast as she could toward the water.

"Jump in!" Violet called out. "You're going to make it!"

Hannah jumped into the water. The Enderman followed as a second Enderman also jumped into the water. Hannah swam back to the shore.

"Creepers and Endermen. This isn't a good sign," lamented Ben.

"We have to find a way to get to Thomas before one of these hostile mobs he's summoned destroys us." Hannah sounded very worried.

Adam offered Hannah some potions to regain her strength. She drank them and thanked him. The group continued on their journey to the Taiga Biome. As the sun began to set, Noah suggested, "Violet, we should build a shelter for the night."

The gang agreed. Violet constructed a house roomy enough to fit everyone inside. As they placed the wood planks on the ground, Violet looked over at Daniel and watched him help construct the house. She couldn't believe that Daniel was actually working with them. There were so many times when Daniel appeared in their makeshift homes and threatened to put them on Hardcore mode. Now he was trying to get them *off* Hardcore mode.

With everyone pitching in, the house was constructed very quickly. Violet entered the house and started to craft beds for her friends.

Once the beds were completed, everyone tucked themselves in.

"Do you hear something?" asked Ben.

"It sounds like someone is screaming for help." Adam listened carefully to the cries in the distance.

Noah suited up in his armor. "I know it's dangerous, but we have to rescue whoever is in trouble."

Dressed in diamond armor, the gang rushed from the house and began searching for the person who was crying for help.

"Zombies!" Hannah called out.

The gang could see zombies lumbering toward them. Two people were fighting them off.

"Help us!" one of the voices cried.

Noah shot an arrow at the undead mob attacking the struggling pair. The gang joined Noah and shot arrows at the zombies, destroying them.

The two strangers called out their thanks, but when Violet and her friends approached the duo, she realized they weren't strangers at all. They were actually old friends.

# 9
# ESCAPE TO
# MOOSHROOM ISLAND

**W**ill!" Violet was excited to see her old treasure hunter friend.

"Trent!" Hannah called out.

"Come with us," Noah insisted. "We built a house. It's too dangerous to be out at night."

Will and Trent paused. Will frowned at Daniel and asked, "Why is Daniel here? He's the enemy!"

"You might not believe this, but Daniel is helping us. We are involved in a serious battle," said Noah. "There's no time to talk. You need to follow us to the house before we get attacked by any more hostile mobs."

Will and Trent accompanied them to the new house.

Will said, "Thanks for letting us spend the night. We are running low on resources and energy."

Trent added, "And there is a rumor going around that the world is set on Hardcore mode."

"That's not a rumor," Noah informed him.

"Seriously?" questioned Will.

"Yes, a griefer named Thomas set the world to Hardcore mode," Daniel told them.

Will and Trent listened to Daniel talk, as Violet crafted two more beds for her friends.

"I want to apologize for my behavior in the past," Daniel told Will and Trent.

Trent replied, "I used to work for you. I know that it's possible to redeem oneself. I did."

"Thanks," said Daniel.

The gang crawled into their beds and went to sleep. When morning arrived, they hopped out of bed, ready to find Thomas. Will and Trent offered the group some of the cake they had in their inventories. Will said, "This is one of the last bits of food we have, but we want to share it with you because you have been so kind to us."

The group thanked them. As they ate the cake, Noah came up with a plan. "I don't think Mooshroom Island is far from here. We should go there because it's free of hostile mobs. We can build lots of homes and set up a new town. If we can't find Thomas, we will need a place to transport the townspeople and the hotel guests. They deserve a place where they will be safe."

"Mooshroom Island is very close by. We passed it yesterday," Will informed them.

The gang exited the house and trekked toward the water. When they reached the shore, they could make out the tip of Mooshroom Island in the distance. Will asked, "Violet, have you ever built a boat?"

Violet had never built a boat, but she said, "I think I can figure it out."

"We each have to make our own boat," Trent reminded them. "We can't travel on the same boat."

The group began to construct small boats to travel to Mooshroom Island. Once finished, they climbed aboard their vessels and set sail to Mooshroom Island. Violet could see the large colorful red mushrooms dotting the terrain. She was excited to visit this scenic island.

The gang docked at Mooshroom Island and explored. A mooshroom was grazing on the mycelium landscape.

"I want to milk the mooshroom. I've never had mooshroom stew," Violet said as she approached the red-and-white passive mob.

Violet grabbed a bowl, got the mooshroom stew, and handed the unusual dish to her friends.

Hannah gulped down the stew and exclaimed, "Tasty!"

"We should start building homes now," Noah reminded the group.

As the gang wandered around the island searching for the perfect spot to build their new community, Ben asked the treasure hunters Will and Trent, "Have you ever met Thomas?"

"No," replied Will. "But I've heard about him. He caused a lot of damage to another village in the Overworld." Will stared at Adam. "You look familiar. Didn't you live in that town?"

"Yes," replied Adam. "But we defeated Thomas in the end."

Will said, "I don't think we should waste our energy building new homes. I really think we should spend our time finding and fighting Thomas."

Violet looked out at the sea as she stood on a hill. She could make out the shore of the mainland they had left behind. She wondered if the hotel had been destroyed yet or if Thomas had returned to their town to attack the townspeople. "Maybe you're right. This wasn't the most well-thought-out plan."

The group passed by huge red mushrooms and headed for the dock.

"Stop here," Violet said before anybody boarded the boats. "This is a quiet spot where we can rest and strategize for a bit. There are no hostile mobs here so we can think without any surprise attacks."

Noah agreed and said, "Everyone, please tell us what you know about Thomas. If we put together all the information we have about him, we might be able to stop him before he destroys the Overworld."

Will said, "I know he likes tunnels."

Adam said, "And he leaves patches of wool wherever he goes."

Daniel said, "He can't be far from the town. He wants to destroy that hotel. He won't be happy until he wrecks it. I think we should head back to town."

"But then we'll be right back where we started," Violet said. She felt a bit annoyed.

"We will be closer to finding him there than we are here." Ben tried to defend the plan. He, too, knew they'd be back at the beginning, but at least they had two more allies to help them now that they were reunited with Will and Trent.

Violet watched her boat floating by the dock. She hated to get back on the boat without a plan of attack, but she was outnumbered. Everyone thought heading back to the hotel was the best idea.

As the gang prepared to climb aboard the boats, Hannah called out, "I see a hole in the ground!"

Violet rushed over to check out Hannah's discovery. Maybe they were closer to finding Thomas than they thought.

# 10
## TUNNELS

**T**his seems to go forever!" Violet called out, as the group traveled through the cavernous tunnel.

"I see a door!" Adam hurried to the door and opened it. The group followed him into a large room.

"This looks like a stronghold." Ben walked around the spacious room, searching for signs of Thomas.

Adam picked up a block of wool and announced, "Thomas was definitely here."

"Yes," a familiar voice called out. A figure emerged from behind a wall. It was Thomas.

"You must take us off Hardcore mode!" demanded Violet.

"Never! I am going to destroy the Overworld!" Thomas screamed and threw a potion of harming on Adam.

Adam's health diminished rapidly. "Help me!" he called out weakly.

Hannah rushed to his side and gave him a potion of healing, while she shouted at Thomas to leave them alone.

Noah charged at Thomas with his diamond sword. "It's over, Thomas!"

Before Noah's sword could strike him, though, Thomas splashed a potion of invisibility on himself and disappeared.

Noah was angry. "He's been pulling the same trick over and over. This guy is a master escape artist."

"We'll never catch him." Violet felt defeated.

Daniel walked around the large room, inspecting the corners. "There's nothing valuable here."

"How do you know?" asked Noah.

Daniel pointed at an empty chest that sat in the corner. "If there was something valuable here, he wouldn't have left."

This made sense to the group. Violet suggested, "I don't think he could have gotten too far. Let's try to find him."

Will agreed. "The potion will wear off soon. We need to pursue him."

They ventured farther into the stronghold and walked up the stairs, entering a room that looked like a library.

"You used to have a place set up in a stronghold," Noah addressed Daniel. "Do you have any idea where he might hide something in this space?"

"He could have command blocks set up anywhere. We really need to find the blocks. We don't even need to find Thomas—the blocks are more important," Daniel said as he opened another door and entered a room with a huge fountain. A stone brick ring dominated the center of the room.

"There isn't anything here," Daniel said. He opened another door, walking into a dark room lit by a single torch placed on the wall.

The gang followed Daniel into the room and noticed a ladder.

"This is a storage room," said Will. "I think there is usually treasure here."

Trent hurried to the ladder and began to climb. "Yes," he called out, "there is a chest in the corner the room up here."

"Don't open it," warned Violet. "It could be booby-trapped."

Trent ignored Violet's warning. "These chests are usually not booby-trapped. It will be fine."

Violet held her breath as Trent opened the chest. He was right. It wasn't booby-trapped.

"Diamonds!" he called out to the gang as he peered into the chest.

Trent climbed down the stairs and handed out diamonds to the group. They placed them in their inventories. As Violet placed the final diamond in her inventory, she noticed a creeper lurking in the corner behind Trent. Before she could utter the words "Watch out," the creeper blew itself up.

*Kaboom!*

"Trent!" Will screamed. But Trent was gone.

"Oh no!" Hannah was devastated.

The group felt sad. Trent was destroyed, and he wouldn't respawn. They stood in silence. There were no words. They missed their friend. The first person to speak was Daniel: "We need to find Thomas. He will pay for this!"

Daniel sprinted toward the door in a rage. He searched the entire stronghold for Thomas. He called out, "Thomas, do you hear me? Where are you hiding? We're going to find you!"

The gang walked with their swords and bows and arrows out ready to attack Thomas, but he was nowhere to be found.

"This is pointless," Will said in frustration. He had just lost his best friend and the group was losing energy in their quest to find Thomas.

They stopped to drink some potions to restore their energy. Adam said, "Look for jail cells."

"Yes," Daniel agreed. "They always have cells in a stronghold."

"We know—you kept us prisoner in one," Noah reminded him.

"And you kept me in a jail cell for ages. So we're even," Daniel retorted.

"Even?" Noah was getting annoyed at Daniel's impudence.

"Guys, this is no time for fighting. We need to find Thomas." Hannah tried to make peace within the group. If they didn't work together, they would never win this battle against Thomas.

"Shh!" Violet called to the others. "I think I hear something."

A muffled noise arose from behind the other iron door in the prison cell.

"It might be Thomas!" Hannah was excited. She wanted this battle to start for real.

Violet carefully opened the iron door and was struck with an arrow. An army of skeletons emerged from behind the door.

"But there aren't skeletons on Mooshroom Island!" Noah was shocked.

"It's Thomas. He's summoning these bony beasts," Violet called out. "He must be the reason they are here!"

Violet's energy was very low. She was struck by another arrow and fumbled with a bottle of potion, hoping she could regain her energy quickly. As she drank the potion, a skeleton shot an arrow at her, and she dropped the potion. Luckily she managed to swallow a small drop, which gave her just enough strength to lunge at the skeleton and destroy it with a blow from her diamond sword.

Adam rushed to her side and gave her some potion. "You'll be okay. We are going to defeat Thomas. It's almost over."

Violet wanted to believe him. She wanted to believe they would be saved and wouldn't be destroyed in this stronghold beneath Mooshroom Island. She thought about the town and the hotel; she missed both places. She yearned for life to be back to normal and to spend the day trading emeralds for meat at Valentino's butcher shop, but she had a battle to win. And sadly, the battle hadn't even begun. Until they found Thomas, or the place where he was using command blocks, and changed the setting off Hardcore mode, they wouldn't be able to go back home and feel safe.

After the final skeleton was destroyed, Violet let out a sigh of relief.

"We're all okay, right?" asked Noah.

The group nodded their heads; they were okay, but they were still sad that Trent was destroyed.

"We have to figure a way out of this stronghold," said Noah.

The group exited the room with the prison cells and walked down a hall. Another door came into view, and Noah opened it, with Violet following closely behind. She looked down at the ground and spotted another block of wool.

"Guys," Violet said in a whisper. "He's here."

Hannah joined Violet. "Are you sure?"

"Yes," she replied and showed the group the block of wool.

"We have to be prepared," Violet said as they opened another door and entered a room with an altar made of stone slabs and a chest.

"Do you think there's treasure in the chest?" asked Ben.

Will walked over to the chest and opened it. "Emeralds!"

"All of this loot is a great find, but it won't do us any good if we're destroyed and don't respawn," remarked Noah.

As they placed the emeralds in their inventories, they heard a voice. Violet looked up and saw someone standing at the door. He pointed his diamond sword at them. She almost passed out in shock. She couldn't believe who was standing there and threatening them to give up their diamonds.

# 11
# DISCOVERIES

**W**ill didn't know if he was happy or horrified. "Trent?" Will called out. He thought he was imagining seeing his friend.

"You're all going to be destroyed!" Trent laughed.

"What?" Daniel asked. "Why are you doing this?"

Noah asked, "How did you respawn?"

Thomas appeared behind Trent and explained, "Trent and I aren't on Hardcore mode."

Will screamed at his friend, "How can you work for Thomas? I trusted you!"

"Never trust a true treasure hunter," Trent replied with a sinister laugh.

"That's not true. *I'm* a treasure hunter, and I can be trusted." Will was upset with his friend and utterly devastated that Trent was working with Thomas.

Noah didn't want to argue. He wanted to destroy the two evildoers who stood by the door. He dashed toward the duo with his sword, but Thomas shielded himself from the blow and struck Noah.

"This is a losing battle. You're on Hardcore mode, and we're not. We will just keep respawning and trying to destroy you until you've run out of resources and have no energy. Just give up," Thomas called to the group.

"Or you can join us and help destroy the Overworld!" added Trent.

"Never!" Violet shouted.

"Why are you doing this?" Will asked Trent.

"When you destroy people in Hardcore mode, you get all of their stuff," explained Trent.

"But soon you'll be the only two people left in the Overworld. If there is nobody left to share the stuff with, what's the point?" Violet was perplexed.

Thomas winced when he heard the word "share." He said, "Share! Who wants to share?"

"Who wants to be alone?" Violet asked.

"I do. When I have all of the treasure from the Overworld, I won't need anybody else. I will have the most loot. I will be the ultimate winner!" Thomas shouted and let out another sinister laugh.

"That doesn't sound like a winner to me. It sounds like a loser." Noah stood next to Violet. "I'd rather have my friends than a bunch of stuff."

"That's why we're different. I don't care about anyone else," Thomas told them.

"Trent," Will said to his old friend, now turned new enemy. "Once Thomas destroys the Overworld, he will set you to Hardcore mode and end your life, too."

Trent looked at Thomas and asked, with a worried expression, "You won't do that, right?"

"Of course not," Thomas replied, but Trent didn't look too sure that Thomas was telling the truth.

"You're pure evil, Thomas. But I actually feel sorry for you," said Violet. "A real person understands the importance of other people and not just things. You're the one who isn't living. Maybe we'll be destroyed and we won't respawn, but at least we had each other, and that's a lot more than you'll ever have in your life."

"You are such a sentimental fool with mixed-up thoughts. You really don't understand how to win the game." Thomas approached Violet and aimed his diamond sword at her chest.

"I don't think we're playing the same game," Violet replied as she backed away from Thomas.

Noah rushed over to his friend and pointed his sword at Thomas. "Take us off Hardcore mode."

"No!" Thomas struck Noah with his sword. The strike was hard and powerful and weakened Noah.

Hannah, Will, Ben, Adam, and Daniel hurried over to Noah and Violet and started to attack Thomas and Trent.

Thomas and Trent fought dirty. They splashed potions on the group, which left the friends extremely tired.

Hannah could barely get a word out, but she wasn't too tired to notice three creepers enter through the door. Thomas and Trent didn't see the green explosive creatures.

*Kaboom!*

But nothing happened.

"We're on Creative mode," Thomas laughed.

"We need to get out of here as fast as we can," Noah told the gang, but he was still feeling the effect of the potion and was extremely weak.

Adam gathered what strength he had and pulled out some bottles of potion from his inventory. The group walked slowly, but finally reached Adam. He handed out the potions. They drank some and felt better.

"We don't have much time," Noah warned them.

"They're about to attack us again," Hannah said as she drank the last of her potion, restoring her energy.

Thomas and Trent sprinted toward the group with their diamond swords. As Adam splashed a potion of harming on them, he also splashed a potion of invisibility on himself and his friends. They used Thomas's trick to escape. Now they had to exit the stronghold before the potion wore off. It was a race against time, and they were hoping they'd win.

# 12
# CRACK THE CODE

**A**dam was the first to call out, "I think I see the room where Thomas is hiding the command blocks." He stopped and looked for the others, but they were all invisible, so he didn't know if they were ahead of or behind him.

"I'm here," Violet said, but they didn't hear from the others. "Let's go into the room. If we can shut off the command blocks, we will have won this battle."

The two of them began to reappear as they walked into the room where Thomas might have set up the command blocks. A man wearing a blue helmet sat in the middle of the room. He looked up at them in surprise. "Who are you?" he asked.

Adam didn't answer. He swung his diamond sword at the man in the blue helmet.

Violet cried out, "Don't! He might be on Hardcore mode and he won't respawn."

"Thanks," the man said to Violet.

"Well, if I do a favor for you, you must return it." She smiled.

"What do I have to do?" he asked.

"Take us off Hardcore mode," demanded Adam.

The man looked confused. "I don't know much about command blocks. Thomas has kept me prisoner and forced me to sit in this room."

"This is most likely where Thomas is controlling the Hardcore setting," Adam replied, and asked if he could put in a new command with a command block.

It was very clear to Adam that this was the place the command blocks were being controlled. "I got it. I switched the setting. We're off Hardcore mode!"

"I'm sorry," the man in the blue helmet told Adam and Violet. "I never knew that I was in charge of such a horrific thing."

"Come with us," Violet said. "We are going to get out of this stronghold. You don't have to be a prisoner anymore."

The blue-helmeted man followed Adam and Violet as they made their way to the exit.

"I'm Jasper," the man said as they hurried down a long hallway.

"Nice to meet you, Jasper. Do you have any idea where an exit might be?" Adam could barely get the words out because he was racing down the hall. He wanted to see daylight. He wanted to emerge on Mooshroom Island and see a large red mushroom.

"I don't know. Thomas trapped me down here so long ago that I have no idea how to escape," Jasper confessed.

The three of them opened doors that lined the hallway, but they were all dead ends. There seemed to be no way out.

"Stop!" a voice called from down the hall.

Violet didn't have to turn around. She knew it was Thomas's voice. The trio ran faster. She opened a door, and they rushed into a room with a staircase and skipped up the stairs.

"Take out your pickaxes," Violet directed Adam and Jasper.

The three of them hit their pickaxes against the roof of the stronghold, trying to break a hole in the ceiling to crawl through.

"I see light!" Adam called out.

Thomas and Trent entered the room and shot arrows at them. An arrow hit Violet and she cried in pain. Adam banged his pickaxe against the ceiling as Violet shot arrows at Thomas and Trent.

"Is the hole big enough to crawl through yet?" Violet asked as she tried to fight off the two evildoers on her own.

"Almost!" Jasper yelled as he and Adam tried again and again to break through the ceiling.

"You have to work faster. I can't hold them off much longer!" Violet was fighting an impossible battle.

Adam handed Violet a potion of harming. "Use this."

Violet splashed the potion on Thomas and Trent. They were temporarily exhausted. Violet used this opportunity to shoot as many arrows as she could at the evil pair.

"Stop!" Thomas called out weakly, but Violet continued to flood Thomas and Trent with a barrage of arrows until they were destroyed.

"Good job," Adam called out as he hit his pickaxe against the ceiling.

"Let me help you guys." Violet took out her pickaxe. "We have to work fast. They are going to respawn soon."

The opening in the ceiling was getting bigger. Finally, Violet pushed her way through the gaping hole and onto the mycelium blocks on Mooshroom Island. They all climbed through the hole and joined Violet on the ground.

"We need to find the others," Violet said as she scanned the landscape of the scenic, rather peaceful island.

"Let's head to the dock. Maybe they are waiting for us," said Adam.

The trio hiked over the hilly island toward the shoreline, passing mooshrooms grazing in the pasture filled with red mushrooms. Once they reached the dock, they could see the boats still floating in the water.

"We have to craft a boat for you," Violet told Jasper.

Adam counted the boats. "Apparently the others are still on the island. We can't leave them here. We must find them."

The trio headed back toward the center of the island. They needed to find their friends. Now that they weren't on Hardcore mode, they weren't as nervous about being destroyed. Violet wondered if Thomas and Trent had defeated her friends and, if so, if they had respawned in the town. Suddenly a terrible thought entered her mind. She didn't even want to think it—it was that awful.

Violet looked at Adam. "What if Thomas and Trent destroyed the others before we were able to take us off Hardcore mode?"

Adam stopped and gasped in alarm at the thought. "That can't be. I hope that isn't the case."

Violet, Adam, and Jasper continued the search for their lost friends. Violet tried to remain hopeful as she roamed around the island calling out to her friends, but they heard no response.

# 13
## GAME OVER

iolet was losing hope. Night was beginning to fall, so Adam suggested they build a small house to shelter in.

"I can use a mushroom and build a mushroom house," Violet declared. Normally she'd be excited to start a new project, but she was worried about her missing friends.

Adam and Jasper helped Violet construct the house. Although she paid attention to building, she also kept an eye out for her friends. She hoped she would see them walking through the landscape toward them.

When the house was finished, the trio went inside and crafted beds. Once they were snugly covered by their blankets, Violet asked, "Do you think our friends are still in the stronghold? We should go back there tomorrow."

Adam confessed, "I'm worried that Thomas put the world back onto Hardcore mode again."

"But we destroyed the command blocks," Jasper reminded him. "And I can tell you that Thomas isn't as powerful as he appears. When I was prisoner, I saw what he really had in his inventory. He is running low on resources. Setting the Overworld to Hardcore mode wasn't easy for him."

Violet hoped Jasper was right. She wondered where her friends were at that very moment. She also thought about Trent and realized how disappointed she was that he had turned so evil. She had trusted him, and he had betrayed them all. When she closed her eyes, she imagined being reunited with her friends. She dreamed of having a picnic with Noah and the gang on Mooshroom Island. They would feast on mooshroom stew and play games without any worries.

Before she knew it, it was morning. The sun was shining and they all sat up in their beds, eating carrots for energy. Soon, Violet realized she didn't have any food left in her inventory.

"I have nothing to eat. I will go find a mooshroom and milk it for stew," she told the others.

Adam offered Violet a carrot. "Take this for now."

As they finished their breakfast, a blast rattled the walls.

"What's that?" asked Adam.

"Sounded like TNT," said Jasper.

The trio dashed out of the house to find where the blast had occurred. They searched for smoke in the sky as they ran through fields of mushrooms and peaceful mooshrooms roaming grassy patches on the island.

Violet spotted Thomas and Trent. They were staring at a hole in the ground. The TNT had left a deep crater.

Violet shot an arrow at Trent, which struck his arm. He turned around and shouted, "Thomas, the enemy is here!"

Violet, Adam, and Jasper hid behind a large mushroom and shot arrows at Thomas and Trent. The evil duo sprinted toward them. Trent shouted, "Game over, guys!"

"Did you set the Overworld back to Hardcore mode? Tell us the truth!" Violet demanded.

"No, we did something worse. And it's over for you, just like it was over for your friends," Thomas laughed.

Violet's heart sunk when she heard Thomas mention her friends. She didn't want to believe they were destroyed; she still hoped to find them somewhere on the island.

"What happened to our friends?" Violet shouted at Thomas.

Thomas smiled and lunged toward Violet with his diamond sword. "Your friends aren't destroyed. But they will be destroyed soon."

"Are they on Hardcore mode?" asked Adam as he shielded himself from Trent's sword.

"Like I'd tell you." Thomas let out a shrill laugh.

Adam took out a potion of harming and splashed it on Thomas. He was weakened. Trent struck Adam with his sword, while Thomas regained his strength.

"You're not going to win this battle. There are three of us and two of you!" Violet shouted as she struck Thomas.

"Two of us?" Thomas replied with a laugh and then called out, "Army activate!"

Violet was shocked and speechless when a group of men in blue helmets crawled out from the tunnel.

"Army—attack!" Thomas ordered again.

The men in blue helmets surged forward. Violet knew she couldn't win this battle. There was nothing left to do but surrender.

"Stop!" she called out to Thomas. "You win. Please just lead us to our friends. We want to say good-bye before we're destroyed."

Thomas smiled. "Haha! You are now my prisoners." He then ordered the soldiers, "Take these people into the cave prison."

Violet, Adam, and Jasper followed the men in the blue helmets down the hole. The men marched the gang through a series of tunnels. Violet didn't recognize this stronghold. She wondered how many strongholds Thomas had discovered on Mooshroom Island.

As they walked down a long corridor, Violet spotted a room filled with wool blocks. When they reached the end of the tunnel, she saw a door. One of the men opened the door and led them into a cave-like room.

Violet called out, "Noah!"

Noah, Hannah, Ben, Will, and Daniel sat in the cave.

Daniel called out, "Help us!"

Noah cried, "We have almost no hearts left. Thomas isn't feeding us."

Hannah screamed, "Attack the men in the blue helmets! It's our only chance to escape."

Ben said quite weakly, "Since we're on Hardcore mode, I guess this is where we say good-bye."

Adam offered the weary group some good news: "We are off Hardcore mode!"

One of the men wearing a blue helmet laughed, "But you're still trapped. Welcome to prison. And now I say, good-bye." The man closed the door and the gang was trapped in the cave.

"How are we going to get out of here?" Violet searched every corner. "Maybe we can dig a hole."

Ben asked, "Does anybody have food? We are starving."

Adam checked his inventory. He discovered he was very low on food, too. He asked Jasper, "How's your food supply?"

Jasper just had a couple of potatoes and an apple. Adam only had milk and chicken.

Violet panicked and groaned, "I don't have any food left in my inventory, either."

Adam calmed her down. "We just ate. So we're fine for a little while. We'll give what we have in our inventories to these guys, so they can restore their energy and help us escape."

Everyone agreed that was a good idea. As the others ate, Violet banged her pickaxe into the cave's ceiling, but no matter how hard she struck, she couldn't make even a dent in the dirt.

"Something is wrong." Violet sounded worried. "I can't break anything with my pickaxe."

# 14
# HELP FROM OLD FRIENDS

Thomas yanked the door open. "Trying to escape?" Violet held her pickaxe in her hand and scoffed at him. "You aren't going to win."

"Maybe the Overworld isn't set to Hardcore mode anymore, but you're on Adventure mode now," Thomas replied.

"Oh, that's why I can't break the blocks." Violet sighed. Now everything made sense.

Adam shot an arrow at Thomas. He shielded himself and laughed. "I let you keep your weapons because they're pointless in this prison. You're not going to get out. There's no escaping!" With those words, Thomas shut the door and the gang was trapped in the cave once again.

Violet felt defeated. Although she was happy to be reunited with her friends, she was upset that she couldn't break through the ceiling and escape. "He's right. Our weapons are pointless. We can't escape, and we have no food. This is our time to say our last good-byes."

"But we're not on Hardcore mode anymore. Maybe we should just destroy each other with the weapons and respawn in the mushroom house," Adam suggested.

Violet couldn't stomach the idea of destroying her friends. She asked Noah and the others, "Where would you respawn?"

Noah pointed at the beds in the corner. "Here."

Adam said, "Violet and Jasper, we can't sleep here."

A cave spider crawled against the wall, and Violet struck the spider with her diamond sword. "See, we *can* use our weapons after all."

Violet paced around the cave; she had to come up with a plan. She needed to defeat Thomas and Trent. She refused to let them win.

"What are we going to do? Any ideas?" Violet asked the group.

Adam suggested they wait to see what Thomas's next move might be.

"That's not a plan!" Noah complained.

"Well, do you have another plan?" Adam demanded.

The group was tired, scared, and beginning to feel overpowered. They were also growing impatient with each other. Nobody had a plan of escape and they began to fight.

Violet put an end to the bickering. "Please. We can't fight. We have to stick together."

"But this is hopeless," Hannah told her.

"Oh no!" Adam shouted, as silverfish began to flood the floor of the cave.

"Thomas must have placed a silverfish spawner in the stronghold," Will said as he used his last bit of energy to destroy the silverfish crawling on the ground.

The group battled the silverfish invasion together. When the last silverfish was destroyed, Noah said, "I'm sure more will spawn soon. This is the end, guys."

Violet looked at the others. "We have to think of something. Adam, can we use one of your potions?"

Adam searched his inventory, but he didn't have many potions left. He just had a few bottles of potions of harming and a potion of invisibility.

"What are we going to do?" Violet called out as more silverfish entered the cave.

Noah grabbed his sword and struck as many silverfish as he could, but the battle seemed pointless. They were just going to lose all their energy battling these insects. They would be destroyed and respawn in the cave. He put his sword down.

"What are you doing?" Ben asked he struck a silverfish.

"Giving up," confessed Noah.

"We never give up," Violet said as she crushed a silverfish.

"Look at what happened to me," Daniel told Noah. "You all fought me so many times, and I never won—you always did. Look how that ended! Now I know better."

"Thomas is different. He put the world on Hardcore mode. He is pure evil." Violet looked at Daniel.

"He's not going to win," Daniel reassured her, but Violet didn't believe him. They had no plan, and they were prisoners.

As Hannah annihilated a cluster of silverfish, she said, "I think I hear something coming from the other side of the door."

"It's probably Thomas with bricks of TNT. He's probably going to blow us up," Violet said weakly.

"No, I hear a voice that sounds really familiar," Hannah said.

The others stood in silence as silverfish crawled around their feet.

Violet replied, "Yes, it sounds like—"

Before she could finish her sentence, the treasure hunters Henry, Lucy, and Max burst through the door.

"You're free!" Lucy called out.

"Come quickly. We need to get you out of here before Thomas respawns," Henry told the group.

"Follow me!" ordered Max.

The gang raced down the hall and toward the light at the end of the tunnel, but when they reached the exit, Thomas and Trent stood blocking their way.

"Where do you think you're going?" Thomas asked and let out another loud sinister laugh.

"Game over, Thomas!" Max said as he struck his sword against him, but Thomas only let out another laugh.

"You can't destroy me," Thomas said, "and you can't escape." He ordered his soldiers to attack.

A sea of men in blue helmets flooded the tunnel and marched the group back toward the cave.

Violet's hope was shattered. As they entered the cave for the second time, she felt there was no possible way to escape, until she heard one of the men in a blue helmet call out, "Ouch!"

Another one of Thomas's soldiers cried, "Help us, Thomas! We are being attacked."

The men in blue helmets were distracted and Violet used this opportunity to run.

"Hurry, this is our chance," Violet shouted to the others.

As they weaved their way through the men in blue helmets and climbed out of the cave-like stronghold, Violet caught a glimpse of an orange person.

# 15
# BATTLE FOR SURVIVAL

**V**iolet never thought she'd see the day when rainbow griefers would save her. As she emerged from the hole, she saw men in blue helmets crawl out and battle a colorful army on Mooshroom Island.

"My army," Daniel said proudly. He called out to the multicolored army, "Good work, soldiers. Keep fighting."

Once all of her friends were safely out of the cave-like stronghold, Violet asked, "Where should we go? Should we help with the battle?"

"We need food and then we can return to battle Thomas," Will said weakly. His food bar was dangerously low.

The group spotted a mooshroom grazing. Violet hurried over to the passive mob and began to milk it. She handed mooshroom stew to everyone.

"When we're done eating, we must help the rainbow army battle Thomas," Lucy told them. "We have to see an end to this battle."

Daniel watched his army fight Thomas and Trent. "This is incredible. I can't believe my army is actually doing something good!"

Violet was amazed when she saw the townspeople and hotel guests running across Mooshroom Island and toward the battle. The villagers were suited up in armor and they carried swords, bows and arrows, and bottles of potion.

"We're here to help!" one of the townspeople called out to the gang.

"The reason you always defeated me," Daniel told his new friends, "is because you have the most powerful resource in the Overworld."

"What is that?" Violet was bewildered.

"You have friends. Look at all these people who want to help you. That is the most powerful resource and gift." Daniel looked out at the never-ending swarm of people who stormed toward Thomas and Trent.

Violet could hear Thomas shout, "I surrender! Please! Stop!"

Noah and the gang rushed to grab Thomas. Noah said, "You give up?"

"Yes, I do." Thomas could barely speak those words; he was exhausted.

Noah was shocked to hear Trent shout, "Thomas, don't surrender! Not yet. It's coming very soon."

"What's coming?" Violet demanded.

"Like I'd tell you," Trent snickered.

Noah held his sword against Trent's chest. "You don't have many hearts left. This is no time to act like this. Tell us what you're planning to do."

They didn't need a response. Within seconds, three Ender Dragons and two Withers were seen flying above the group.

Everyone began to battle the invasion of flying hostile mobs. Wither skulls shot through the sky like rain. Ender Dragons let out deafening roars in unison. The gang was under full attack! Thomas and Trent simply laughed and watched the battle. Violet didn't want them to escape, so she held her sword against Trent, and Adam stood by Thomas and aimed his bow and arrow at this chest.

"You'll never win!" Thomas cried out.

Violet marched Thomas back into the cave. "You had better take the Overworld off Adventure mode right now!" she demanded.

"Never!" Thomas declared.

Adam marched Trent into the cave, following Violet and Thomas. Adam said, "We are going to use command blocks to put you two on Hardcore mode."

"No, don't do that!" Thomas pleaded.

"Once you are on Hardcore mode, with one strike, you'll be destroyed. Your energy is very low and you are on an island where everyone wants to destroy you because of all the evil you've brought to the Overworld." Violet pointed her sword as she spoke to Thomas.

Adam used command blocks to set Thomas and Trent onto Hardcore mode. "There! Now do you think I was joking?"

Thomas panicked. "You aren't serious!"

"Yes, I am," Adam replied.

"Stop summoning these hostile mobs!" Violet demanded as she plunged her sword into Thomas and he lost another heart.

"Okay, okay!" Thomas cried. "I'll do it. I'll stop summoning them."

Adam took Thomas and Trent off Hardcore mode.

Thomas led Violet and Adam to a room where he had been summoning the beasts and stopped calling for more. "I can't get rid of the ones I've already sent here, though."

"Then you will help us battle them," Violet told him.

"But I don't have very much energy left," said Thomas.

"You should have thought about that before you terrorized this entire island with flying devils." Adam was annoyed. He marched Thomas outside, where a serious battle against the Ender Dragons and the Withers was taking place in the skies above Mooshroom Island.

Adam shot an arrow at an Ender Dragon and it let out a loud roar. Violet was surprised when someone handed her a snowball.

She looked over and said, "Thank you, Thomas."

Thomas and Violet threw snowballs at the Ender Dragon until it was destroyed. The townspeople obliterated the other Ender Dragons, and then there were only two Withers left flying through the sky, shooting wither skulls at them. Thomas threw a snowball at one Wither, but he couldn't avoid being hit by the wither skull. He was destroyed.

"Where will he respawn?" Adam asked Trent.

"In the cave," Trent replied.

"Show us," Violet said.

The three hurried to the respawning point. Violet didn't trust Thomas, and she wanted to be present the minute he reappeared. Trent led them to the room with two beds, where he and Thomas had last slept. Thomas respawned in the bed. He woke up and saw Violet standing in front of him.

"I will go back and help you battle the Wither," Thomas said as he got up from the bed. "I'm sorry. I really am."

Violet was happy to hear his apology, but she wanted to see Thomas defeat the Wither in person. He had summoned these beasts, so he had to destroy them and save everyone trying to battle these evil creatures. The group ran for the exit. As they reached the light, the Wither flew close to them and struck Violet with a skull. She was destroyed.

Violet respawned in the bed at the mushroom house. She looked out the window and saw the people battling the Wither. There was only one Wither left—the other must have been destroyed while she, Adam, Trent, and Thomas were in the cave. She was shocked to see Thomas standing outside the mushroom house. Adam stood next to him.

"Thomas has agreed to come back to town with us and stay in the jailhouse," Adam told her.

Violet watched as the last Wither was destroyed. "It's finally over." She breathed a sigh of relief.

# 16
# IN THE MINE

I t's over," Thomas announced to the crowd of townspeople, hotel guests, rainbow griefers, and men in blue
helmets. "The Overworld is back on Survival mode. I
apologize for all the trouble I have caused."

Adam said, "Did you take us off Adventure mode?"

Thomas gasped, "No, I must do that!"

The crowd wasn't satisfied with Thomas's apology,
however. They wanted Thomas to pay a price for all the
chaos he had caused in the Overworld. Many people had
been destroyed and would never respawn.

A townsperson called out, "Sorry isn't good enough!"

Violet stood in front of the people and explained,
"Thomas and Trent are coming back to our town. They
are going to be locked up in the jail."

The townspeople and hotel guests were happy that
Thomas and his evil sidekick were going to be trapped
in a jail and couldn't cause any more trouble. They were
also glad to leave Mooshroom Island and so they jogged

down to the shore, hopped on their boats, and headed back to their homes and the hotel. The only people who remained on Mooshroom Island were Violet and her friends.

Violet said to Thomas, "I think you'd better lead us to the command blocks and take us off Adventure mode."

Thomas led the group down the hole and into a cavernous stronghold. They passed through a dimly lit tunnel. It was very quiet in the stronghold, and Violet couldn't believe that just minutes earlier an intense battle between the men in blue helmets and the rainbow griefers had taken place there.

"Here they are," Thomas said as they entered a room holding the command blocks. He quickly set them back to Survival mode.

"It's time to take you back to our town. I am going to rebuild the jail, and you will stay there forever," Violet told Thomas.

Thomas wasn't too pleased, but he knew there was no other option. He couldn't be a griefer—he had to go to jail.

The group headed toward the shore. As they hiked down a hill, Noah spotted a mine.

"Should we mine for diamonds?" Will sounded excited.

"Of course!" Lucy replied quickly. She was always up for an adventure and now that they were all safe, she wanted to do fun things again.

The group put on their helmets, grabbed their pick-axes, and advanced into the dark mine.

"Thomas and Trent, we are keeping an eye on you. You can't escape," Adam warned the griefers.

"I won't. I promise," replied Thomas.

"I'll be good, too," added Trent.

Lucy said, "I've heard you promise not to grief before. I'll believe it when I see it."

"Don't worry, they'll both be in jail soon," Violet reminded her as they banged their pickaxes against the ground and searched for diamonds.

"And don't try to escape from the jail," Daniel warned Thomas. "It can backfire on you, like it did on me."

"I was the one helping you escape," joked Thomas.

"And look how well that worked out," replied Daniel.

Violet reflected on Daniel's comment and said, "In a weird way, it did work out. It taught you that you shouldn't grief any more."

Daniel smiled. "You're right," and then he called out to the group, "Diamonds! I found diamonds!"

"This was a great idea. I'm so glad we went mining for diamonds," Ben exclaimed as he placed diamonds safely in his inventory.

"Now we have something to trade when we get back to town," added Hannah.

"Shh!" Violet whispered. "I hear someone!"

The group expected to see another hostile mob and readied themselves for an attack, but then they remembered hostile mobs don't spawn on Mooshroom Island, and Thomas wasn't summoning any more, either.

"Who could it be?" asked Hannah nervously.

Violet grabbed her sword and crept toward the exit to see who was making noise in the mine.

Violet spotted two people in the distance. Noah aimed his bow and arrow at the approaching figures, but Lucy screamed, "Stop! Don't! I know them!"

# 17
# IT'S A GAME

S teve!" Lucy called out.

"Kyra!" Max was happy to see his old friend.

Noah put his bow and arrow away. Henry introduced the group to his friends Steve and Kyra.

Steve was shocked to see Thomas in the mine. "What are *you* doing here?" he asked.

Lucy explained to Violet and her friends about the time Thomas had blown up Steve's wheat farm.

Violet shook hands with Steve and said, "We are bringing Thomas back to our town and placing him and his friend Trent in jail."

"That's great," Steve replied and added, "I know who you are, Violet. You are a master builder. I've seen some of your work in the Overworld. You're very talented."

Steve was also a skilled builder and had once taken part in a building competition on Mooshroom Island.

"Thanks!" Violet was pleased to hear that others respected her work.

"There are diamonds in this mine, Steve," Lucy informed him.

Kyra was excited to mine for diamonds. "Great, I can't wait to fill my inventory with diamonds."

Violet told everyone, "I think it's time we return to our town. We have enough diamonds in our inventories, and we need to take Thomas and Trent to jail."

Will shook his head at Trent and lamented, "I can't believe you turned evil. Now you have to pay the price."

Trent stared at Will and just uttered, "I'm sorry."

Lucy wished the others a good trip home. "I think we're going to stay here with Steve and Kyra."

Will said, "I'm also going to stay and mine here."

Violet was sad to say good-bye to Will, but she knew she'd see him again.

What was left of the group made their way toward the shoreline. Thomas and Trent didn't have boats. They had used boats to get to Mooshroom Island and then destroyed them so nobody would discover they were there. Now they needed to build new boats, but didn't have any wood in their inventories.

Violet offered to build boats for Thomas and Trent. "You need one. There is no way we are going to let you escape or stay here on this beautiful island. You don't deserve to stay here."

Once the boats were constructed and everyone had climbed into them, they started their journey over the deep blue water and back to the village.

# 18

# FRIENDS AND FIREWORKS

The gang docked on the sandy shore by the hotel and made their way into town. Valentino the Butcher greeted them when they arrived. "Hi, everyone. We have a surprise for you."

Violet strolled into the center of town and stopped. "Wow, you rebuilt the jailhouse. How fantastic!"

Noah marched Thomas and Trent straight into the jailhouse. Daniel followed and asked, "Do you want me to go back to my old cell, too?"

Violet paused to think. "I think you should stay in the town, but you don't have to spend any more time in jail."

Daniel was pleased. "I'd be honored if you built a house for me in this town so I can stay for a long time."

Violet smiled. "I'd love to do that for you."

A group of rainbow griefers approached Daniel. He looked at them and gave out new instructions: "The rainbow griefer army has disbanded. Please feel free to pick any skin and wear it."

The griefers cheered and gave up their colorful skins for ones they chose for themselves.

Violet announced, "We will finally celebrate the grand re-opening of the hotel. I'm going to go over there and repair the damage and then we can hold the festivities."

Valentino said, "The hotel guests already repaired the damage—the hotel looks brand new."

Violet loved hearing this news. She couldn't wait to party at the hotel with her friends. "Tonight, we will have a celebration, complete with fireworks."

Thomas and Trent peered out from the windows of their jail cells. They wouldn't be able to enjoy the fireworks display; they would spend their days in the jailhouse.

Daniel asked, "Can I attend the fireworks show? The last time you had one at the Olympic games, I destroyed it."

"We remember that," said Noah.

"But we defeated you and had another fireworks display after that. You could never end our celebrations," Violet told him.

Daniel said, "I can't believe I'm actually going to one of your celebrations as a guest and not as an enemy trying to destroy you."

It was getting dark, so the group hurried to the hotel to watch the fireworks. Everyone placed torches around the hotel to stop hostile mobs from spawning and destroying the grand re-opening celebration.

Before the fireworks started, the gang put on a great feast. As Daniel ate a piece of chicken, he said to the group, "I know I keep apologizing for my behavior, but I can't believe I tried to destroy one of these celebrations. They're so much fun."

A man in a brown suit came up to Daniel. "I used to be an orange griefer in your army. I just want you to know how much I hated griefing, and I am so happy to see you are a good guy now. It makes the Overworld a better place."

Daniel looked at the man and apologized. "I'm sorry I trapped you and made you join an evil army. I'm glad that you were able to choose your own skin. You look great."

Violet and Noah watched as Daniel talked to the ex-griefer. Violet said, "Noah, it is wonderful that order is restored in the Overworld. I'm so relieved. Now we can finally relax, and I can build so many things without fear of them being destroyed."

"Yes," Noah said, "but we always have to be on the lookout. You never know when another griefer might attack us."

"That's true, but I try to look at the bright side of things." She smiled.

Hannah and Ben hurried over. "We just checked on Thomas and Trent. They are still in the jail."

"Great!" exclaimed Violet.

Daniel strolled over to the group and offered them cake. Violet took a piece and thanked him.

"Look up!" Violet told Daniel.

"What? Did somebody summon the Ender Dragon?" he questioned nervously.

"No, silly. The fireworks are about to begin." Violet pointed to a colorful display of lights flashing across the dark sky.

The crowd cheered. It was a wonderful, festive night in the Overworld. In the morning, Violet would help rebuild any additional damage caused by the battle, but for now, she was just happy celebrating the newly rebuilt hotel. She imagined how many fun activities would take place there.

Someone called out a warning that zombies were approaching. Although the streets were brightly lit with torches, the zombies were ripping doors off buildings in the town. Violet worried they'd rip the door off the jailhouse. She called for the officials to halt the fireworks show.

The gang battled the invading zombies. It seemed very easy after battling Thomas, Trent, and the army of men in blue helmets. After the last zombie was defeated, Violet decided to check the jailhouse. Luckily, Thomas and Trent were still there.

The group returned to the hotel, and the fireworks display continued. Violet glanced over at her friends and Daniel and realized that people can change. She hoped Thomas and Trent would one day be able to watch a fireworks show with the gang and be a part of a celebration instead battling the town.

The red and gold fireworks lit up the night sky like giant sparklers. The crowd cheered. It was a stunning and celebratory night in the Overworld.

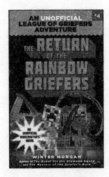

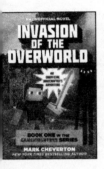

# LIKE OUR BOOKS
# FOR MINECRAFTERS?

Then check out other novels
from Sky Pony Press.

**Pack of Dorks**
BETH VRABEL

**Boys Camp:
Zack's Story**
CAMERON DOKEY,
CRAIG ORBACK

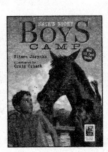

**Boys Camp:
Nate's Story**
KITSON JAZYNKA,
CRAIG ORBACK

**Letters from an
Alien Schoolboy**
R. L. ASQUITH

**Just a Drop of
Water**
KERRY O'MALLEY
CERRA

**Future Flash**
KITA HELMETAG
MURDOCK

**Sky Run**
ALEX SHEARER

**Mr. Big**
CAROL AND MATT
DEMBICKI

Available wherever books are sold!